Caste No Bar

By

Mandeep Kaur

In the vibrant city of Shergarh, nestled amidst the golden fields of Punjab, India, where the aroma of spicy samosas wafted through narrow alleyways and the vibrant colors of traditional bazaars painted the streets as street vendors prepared their stalls for the day's trade, the lives of Nina and Arun unfolded against the backdrop of ancient customs and modern aspirations. The sun rose with a promise of a bustling day ahead. Amidst this lively scene, stood Nina, a young woman whose spirit danced with the rhythm of the city. Her almond eyes, framed by dark lashes, sparkled with determination each morning, as the first rays of the sun painted the sky with hues of crimson and gold, Nina embarked on her journey aboard the direct train to Delhi Central City.

As the train chugged along its well-worn tracks, Nina's gaze wandered beyond the confines of the carriage, seeking solace in the ever-changing canvas of the sky. Wispy clouds, tinged with shades of gray, drifted lazily overhead, casting fleeting shadows on the sprawling fields below. In the distance, the towering skyscrapers of Delhi rose like sentinels against the horizon, their glass facades reflecting the morning light in a dazzling display.

Clad in the vibrant colors of her traditional yellow shalwar kameez, Nina stood out amidst the sea of commuters, her scarf billowing in the breeze like a flag of defiance against the monotony of urban life. With each passing moment, the rhythmic clatter of the train became a comforting backdrop to her thoughts, a steady rhythm that mirrored the beating of her heart.

It was on one such morning, as the city stirred to life around her, that Nina's gaze met that of a handsome stranger, his dark eyes alight with curiosity. Arun, as she would later come to know him, exuded an aura of quiet confidence that drew her in like a moth to a flame. Against the backdrop of the bustling train carriage, their chance encounter felt like a scene plucked from the pages of a Bollywood romance, two souls destined to meet amidst the chaos of modern life.

As Nina stole glances in Arun's direction, she felt a flutter of excitement stir within her, a sense of anticipation tinged with apprehension. Nina was a nursing student and Arun is a IT Programer and that was why they commuted on the train daily.

In the intricate tapestry of Indian culture, where tradition and modernity coexisted in a delicate balance, their budding romance felt both exhilarating and forbidden, a forbidden fruit ripe for the plucking.

Despite her yearning to engage with the intriguing stranger, Nina's reserved nature held her back, her upbringing instilling in her a sense of propriety and decorum. And so, as the train rattled along its familiar route, she contented herself with stolen glances and fleeting smiles, each moment a precious treasure in the tapestry of their burgeoning connection.

As the days turned into weeks, Nina and Arun's clandestine meetings blossomed into whispered conversations and stolen moments of connection, their bond deepening with each passing day. Yet, looming over their newfound happiness were the shadows of tradition and expectation, societal norms that threatened to tear them apart.

But amidst the chaos of the city, amidst the ever-changing sky and the bustling streets below, Nina and Arun found solace in each other's arms, their love a beacon of hope amidst the uncertainty of their future. And as they embarked on their journey together, hand in hand, they knew that no matter what obstacles lay ahead, their love would endure, a testament to the power of love to conquer all.

Arun, with his dusky complexion and piercing eyes that mirrored the depths of the night sky, hailed from a humble background , born into a lower caste family whose roots ran deep in the fertile soil of the Punjab region. Despite his family's education and achievements, societal expectations weighed heavily upon him, dictating that he remain within the confines of his caste, forever bound by the chains of tradition.

In stark contrast, Nina, with her fair skin and graceful demeanor, belonged to a higher caste, her lineage traced back through generations of respected community leaders and scholars. Yet, despite the privileges afforded by her station, she found herself ensnared in the rigid hierarchy of Indian society, where love dared not cross the boundaries of caste and class.

Their chance encounter aboard the bustling Metro train was a collision of worlds, a fleeting moment that defied the constraints of tradition and expectation. As they exchanged furtive glances amidst the throngs of commuters, a spark ignited between them, setting aflame the embers of forbidden desire.

Determined to defy the dictates of their caste-bound society, Nina embarked on a journey of self-discovery and sacrifice, her heart torn between the obligations of filial duty and the yearnings of her own soul. Each stolen moment with Arun became a testament to their shared defiance, a silent rebellion against the suffocating grip of societal norms.

Yet, as their love blossomed amidst the chaos of the city, so too did the shadows of doubt and fear, casting a pall over their burgeoning romance. Nina, torn between her devotion to Arun and the expectations of her family, wrestled with the weight of her decision, her heart a battleground of conflicting emotions.

She did not feel comfortable going to any of her family members for help for fear of shame she may bring to the family's reputation. She then remembered that her father had a trusted Pandit, a pandit is a trusted fortune teller commonly used in India. People in the Indian culture almost live their life around what advice a pandit gives.

In her hour of need, Nina turned to the wisdom of the ancients, seeking guidance from the revered Pandit whose words held sway over the fate of generations. With bated breath, she confided in him her deepest desires and darkest fears, trusting in his insight to illuminate the path ahead.

As she stepped into the hallowed sanctuary of the Pandit's prayer room, the air thick with the scent of sandalwood and incense, Nina felt a sense of calm wash over her. Here, in this sacred space where time stood still, she laid bare her soul before the wise old sage, seeking solace in his age-old wisdom.

With each word uttered in hushed tones, the Pandit peered into the depths of Nina's soul, his ancient eyes seeing truths that lay hidden beneath the surface. Through the art of palmistry and the ancient science of birth charts, he unraveled the threads of destiny that bound Nina to her past and shaped her future. Furthermore, he also explained to her about birthstones and how every person each had a unique birthstone that had qaulities that protect them from evil.

As the session drew to a close, Nina emerged from the prayer room with a newfound sense of clarity and purpose, her heart lighter than it had been in days. Armed with the Pandit's guidance and the strength of her love for Arun, she knew that no obstacle could stand in the way of their forbidden love, a love that transcended the boundaries of caste and culture, a love that would endure for eternity."Hello, Uncle Ji," she said in a quiet and nervous voice.

"Welcome," he said, "It's been too long since I have seen you."

"How is the family doing?" he asked.

"They are all well," she said, "and yes, it has been too long since we have met."

"How is my little brother Sunjay?" He asked.

"Papa is good, thanks," she said.

"How can I help you, my child?" The Pandit asked.

"Something in your voice told me that you were nervous about something when you called me yesterday," the Pandit continued.

"Yes, I am very burdened," she explained, "You must know that I am engaged to Jatinder and my wedding is in two months." The Pandit nodded and said, "Yes, the family did share that with me a few months ago. Is there a problem with this marriage?

Nina nodded and said, "Yes, there is." Her heart began to beat fast again as she began to tell the pandit her problem.

As the sun dipped below the horizon, casting a warm glow over the quaint village of Chittorgarh, Nina found herself sitting in the humble abode of Pandit Ram, a revered figure in the community known for his wisdom and

4

spiritual guidance. The scent of incense filled the air, mingling with the soft strains of devotional music playing in the background.

Pandit Ram, clad in traditional attire befitting his esteemed role, wore a pristine white dhoti intricately pleated and draped with precision, symbolizing purity and piety. Over his broad shoulders, he donned a saffron-colored angavastram, its rich hue representing the sacred fire of knowledge that he faithfully tended to. Around his neck, strands of rudraksha beads adorned his chest, a testament to his devout devotion to Lord Shiva.

After Nina, resplendent in vibrant traditional attire, had poured her heart out, Pandit Ram, with his flowing white beard and gentle demeanor, gestured for her to place her palms on his, saying, "Let me delve into the depths of your fate, my child. I will do my utmost to ease your burdens."

Nina complied, her hands trembling slightly as the pandit scrutinized her palms with a furrowed brow, his forehead adorned with a prominent bindi symbolizing his deep connection to the divine. Meeting her gaze with a solemn expression, he spoke, "What troubles your heart, dear one?"

"Uncle Ji, I stand at a crossroads. I need to know if my parents will embrace my choice to follow my heart, rather than conforming to their wishes for an arranged marriage," Nina confided, her voice tinged with uncertainty.

The pandit sighed softly, his eyes reflecting the weight of his wisdom. "I cannot predict their reaction with certainty, but I sense a period of turbulence and discord looming within your family."

"And when will this tumult arise?" Nina inquired, her heart racing with apprehension.

"In this current decade of your life," came the cryptic response, imbued with the mysticism of ancient divination practices passed down through generations.

"And what form will this strife take?" she pressed, her breath catching in her throat.

"That, my child, remains veiled from my sight," he admitted, his voice tinged with regret.

Nina's heart sank, her thoughts consumed by the specter of familial conflict. "That is the answer I feared. My parents will likely resist my choice, insisting on the path they have chosen for me," she lamented, her voice trembling with emotion.

"I wish I could offer you solace, but I must speak the truth. Should you proceed with the arranged marriage, you may find yourself at odds with your deepest desires," the pandit confessed, his words carrying the weight of centuries of spiritual wisdom. "I could intercede on your behalf with your parents, if you so desire. Our bond spans decades, and they hold my counsel in high regard."

"But would my seeking guidance from you instead of them only deepen their resentment?" Nina pondered aloud, her brow furrowed with concern. "Thank you, Uncle Ji, for your honesty. It is the clarity I sought."

The pandit nodded solemnly, his eyes shimmering with compassion. As Nina's tears began to flow, he enveloped her in a comforting embrace, his touch a balm to her wounded spirit. "My child, life is a tapestry woven with threads of joy and sorrow. We must embrace them both, for they are but steps on the path ordained by the divine," he reassured her, his words infused with the timeless wisdom of the Vedas.

"Nina, allow me to fashion a gemstone for you," he continued, his tone imbued with solemnity. "Though it may not vanquish all your troubles, it can serve as a conduit for positive energy, guiding you towards the light in even the darkest of times."

With a nod of gratitude, Nina accepted the offer, finding solace in the pandit's words and the promise of a brighter tomorrow guided by the wisdom of the ancients. And as she left the sanctum of Pandit Ram's dwelling, the echoes of his words lingered in her heart, a beacon of hope illuminating the path ahead.

As the days passed, Nina found herself immersed in the soothing rhythm of daily prayers, as advised by Pandit Ram. Each morning, she would rise before the break of dawn, lighting incense sticks and offering fragrant flowers at the altar adorned with images of gods and goddesses. The melodious chants of ancient mantras filled the air, wrapping her in a cocoon of spiritual solace.

One morning, as Nina prepared to leave for her daily prayers, she was surprised to find Pandit Ram waiting for her at the train station, a serene smile adorning his weathered face. In his hands, he held a delicate emerald necklace, its verdant hues shimmering in the morning light.

"Wear this every day, my child," he explained, his voice soft yet resolute. "Let it serve as a beacon of hope amidst your trials."

Overwhelmed with gratitude, Nina accepted the necklace, her heart heavy with the weight of her impending decision. "Thank you, Uncle Ji," she whispered, her voice choked with emotion. With a tender kiss on her forehead, Pandit Ram reassured her, his eyes reflecting the unwavering faith he held in the divine plan.

"Stay strong, my dear. Know that I am always here for you," he said, his gaze turning towards the heavens as if seeking guidance from the celestial realms.

Despite his comforting words, Nina's heart remained burdened with uncertainty. As she boarded the train, her thoughts drifted to Arun, the man she loved, and the daunting choice that lay ahead.

Days turned into weeks, and with each passing moment, Nina felt the weight of her dilemma grow heavier. Finally, on a rainy stormy day, she and Arun knew they could delay their decision no longer. With hearts heavy with both excitement and dread, they resolved to forge their own path together.

That evening, as Nina returned home, she packed her belongings, her hands trembling as she held the treasured items passed down from her grandmother. Among them, a golden necklace caught her eye, its intricate design evoking memories of happier times.

As she fastened the necklace around her neck, tears welled in Nina's eyes, her mind plagued by doubts and fears. Am I doing the right thing? Will I ever find peace with my decision?

But amidst the turmoil, a quiet resolve began to take root within her. With trembling hands and a heart heavy with sorrow, Nina knew that she could no longer deny her truth. Stepping into the family room, she summoned the courage to confront her parents, her voice trembling as she spoke of her wishes and desires.

Though the journey ahead was fraught with uncertainty, Nina knew that she could no longer live a life dictated by others' expectations. With her faith as her guiding light, she embarked on a journey of self-discovery, trusting in the wisdom of the divine to illuminate her path.

"Beta, what is wrong?" her mother asked.

"Mummy and Daddy, I need to tell you something," Nina said in her quiet sobbing voice.

"What is it child?" her father asked in a worried and loud voice.

Nina continued, "I am not going to get married."

"What!" her parents yelled.

"What are you saying?" her mother asked.

"Did something happen?" her father asked.

The living room exuded an air of understated elegance, its walls adorned with ornate tapestries and shelves lined with cherished family mementos. Intricately patterned rugs sprawled across the polished wooden floor, their vibrant hues casting a kaleidoscope of colors in the sun-drenched space. Embroidered cushions adorned the plush sofa, inviting guests to sink into their soft embrace as they engaged in earnest conversation.

Amidst this picturesque setting, Nina sat, a vision of distress amidst the opulent surroundings. Her tear-streaked face betrayed the turmoil within, her delicate features etched with sorrow as she grappled with the weight of her emotions. Across from her, Sunjay and Sunita occupied regal armchairs, their expressions a testament to their concern for their daughter's well-being.

Sunita's eyes shimmered with unshed tears as she reached out to comfort Nina, her touch a gentle reassurance amidst the storm. "Nina beta," she murmured, her voice a soothing melody laced with worry, "please, help us understand."

Struggling to compose herself, Nina lifted her head, her gaze meeting her parents' with unwavering resolve. "I've met someone," she confessed, her voice trembling with emotion, "and I cannot turn away from the love we share."

Sunjay's countenance darkened with disbelief, his features a mask of paternal disappointment. "But we've made arrangements for your wedding," he protested, his voice tinged with frustration. "How can you betray our trust in this manner?" Sunjay yelled "The boy is of a lower caste and we are of a higher Jatt caste, the two have no common ground. We will not allow any such marriage to take place. Jatinder your chosen husband is who you will marry. The punjabi cultures whole foundation is within the caste system. You will not disgrace our good family name with your foolish nonsense. Sunita have you taught your daughter nothing??" he yelled.

Beside him, Sunita's expression softened with empathy as she turned to Nina, her voice a gentle plea for understanding. "How can you be sure of this person, beta? You've only known them for a few weeks," she reasoned, her maternal concern palpable.

Yet, Nina's resolve remained unyielding as she met her parents' gaze, her voice echoing with determination. "I understand your concerns, but I cannot deny the love that burns within my heart," she insisted, her words a fervent declaration of her truth.

Sunjay's frustration simmered beneath the surface, his tone laced with authority as he sought to impose his will. "We know what's best for you," he asserted, his words carrying the weight of paternal authority. "Your fiancé comes from a respectable family, with a stable career and financial security. You cannot jeopardize your future for fleeting emotions."

Sunita's eyes brimmed with tears as she reached out to her daughter, her voice trembling with emotion. "Nina beta, we have invested so much in this alliance," she implored, her words a poignant plea for reason. "We cannot risk it all based on a whim."

In the days that followed, Nina grappled with her inner turmoil, seeking solace in the sanctuary of her prayers. Each morning, as the first light of dawn filtered through her window, she found herself torn between duty and desire, her heart heavy with the weight of her decision.

One morning, as the gentle rays of sunlight danced across her bedroom floor, Nina was roused from her reverie by a soft knock on her door. It was Sunita, her expression a mixture of solemnity and resolve. "Nina, please come downstairs," she urged, her voice tinged with urgency. "Your father and I need to speak with you."

Descending the stairs with trepidation, Nina braced herself for the conversation that awaited her, her heart fluttering with anticipation. She smoothed down her hair with trembling fingers, the familiar weight of her emerald necklace a comforting presence against her skin.

In the family room, Sunjay and Sunita awaited her, their expressions grave yet filled with a quiet determination. Sunjay gestured for her to take a seat, his voice steady yet tinged with emotion. "We have deliberated, Nina," he began, his words measured and deliberate. "And we have reached a decision."

Tears welled in Nina's eyes as she listened to her father's words, her heart overflowing with gratitude for their understanding. Sunita's voice quivered with emotion as she reached out to her daughter, her touch a silent affirmation of their unwavering love. "We respect your wishes, beta," she murmured, her words a tender reassurance amidst the storm.

And then, in a moment of vulnerability, her parents revealed a long-kept secret, laying bare their own struggles and sacrifices for love. Sunjay and Sunita recounted their life story of courage, resilience and love. Nina discovered that her parents marriage had faced a lot of backlash from her father's family as he was more educated. Sunjay was a doctor while Sunita was only a teacher. Sunjay's family believed that they were not a good fit and hence they had no choice but to elope. As they recounted their clandestine romance, Nina's heart swelled with a newfound understanding of their unconditional love, their shared history a testament to the enduring power of love in the face of adversity.

In the tranquil embrace of their tastefully adorned home, the ambiance was one of subdued elegance, with the warm glow of intricately designed lamps casting delicate shadows across the spacious living room. Rich tapestries adorned the walls, telling stories of generations past, while embroidered cushions offered respite upon plush sofas, their soft textures inviting one to linger in comfort.

Nina's return home from the hospital was greeted with a mixture of relief and anticipation, her parents, Sunjay and Sunita, waiting with open arms at the threshold. As she stepped through the door, the familiar scent of home enveloped her, a comforting embrace after a long day's work.

"How was your day, child?" Sunjay inquired, his voice tinged with concern. Nina's response was punctuated by a weary sigh, the weight of her responsibilities evident in her weary expression. "Busy, as usual," she murmured, her words a reflection of the demands of her profession.

Sunita, her mother, seemed particularly overwhelmed, her breaths coming in short, hurried bursts. Yet, amidst the hustle and bustle of daily life, the promise of a shared meal offered a moment of respite. "Dinner is ready," they announced, their voices infused with warmth and hospitality. "Let's eat together, later."

As they gathered around the dining table, the aroma of aromatic spices filled the air, mingling with the laughter and conversation that flowed freely between them. Yet, beneath the surface, a sense of unease lingered, a silent reminder of the impending conversation that loomed over them like a shadow.

In the days that followed, Nina's parents found themselves grappling with the weight of an uncertain future, their thoughts consumed by the delicate balance of tradition and individual autonomy. Sunjay, ever the patriarch, bore the burden of responsibility with a heavy heart, his brow furrowed in contemplation as he sought a path forward.

"What troubles you, papa?" Nina ventured, her concern evident in the furrow of her brow. "Is it Arun and his family? Do you not approve?"

Sunjay's response was measured, his words laden with the weight of parental concern. "No, they seem like good people," he conceded, his voice tinged with uncertainty. "But it is the matter of explaining...this situation...to Jatinder and his family that weighs heavily on my mind."

Sunita, ever the voice of reason, offered her own perspective, her words a soothing balm amidst the turmoil. "We must approach this with humility and honesty," she urged, her voice filled with quiet resolve. "Let us take a few days to gather our thoughts, and then we shall face this challenge together."

And so, in the quiet moments that followed, Nina's parents found solace in each other's company, drawing strength from the bonds of love and family that bound them together. As they navigated the complexities of tradition and modernity, they found themselves united in their commitment to honor their daughter's wishes, while also respecting the traditions that had shaped their lives.

In the midst of it all, Pandit Ji's visit served as a poignant reminder of the role that faith and tradition played in their lives. His words, delivered with gentle wisdom, resonated deeply within their hearts, offering reassurance amidst the uncertainty that lay ahead.

As the evening drew to a close and their guests departed, Sunjay sank wearily onto the sofa, his thoughts consumed by the challenges that lay ahead. Yet, amidst the uncertainty, there was a glimmer of hope, a belief that with faith and humility, they would find a way forward.

And so, as they sat together in the quiet embrace of their home, Nina's family found strength in each other's love, their hearts filled with the belief that no matter what trials lay ahead, they would face them together, united in their shared journey of love, faith, and family.

A few days had passed and Nina's parents were waiting for her to come home from the hospital. They greeted her at the door with a hug. "How was your day child?" her father asked. "It was nice," she said. "But very busy as usual," she explained. Sunita seemed to be overwhelmed by something as she was breathing very hard. "Dinner is made," they said, "We are going to eat later."

"Are you going somewhere?" Nina asked. "Yes, we are going to meet Jatinder tonight and explain everything to him. Don't worry. We will take care of the matter," her father said. Nina looked worried and nodded. "We are going to meet outside their home at a restaurant," her father said. "Okay daddy," Nina said, "I hope it goes okay."

Sunjay and Sunita found themselves immersed in the hustle and bustle of Alipur, a vibrant city steeped in history and tradition. As they made their way through the labyrinthine streets, the din of the city faded into the background, replaced by the quiet anticipation that hung heavy in the air.

Their destination lay in a secluded corner of the city, where time seemed to stand still amidst the crumbling facades of ancient buildings. The restaurant they sought was nestled amidst this forgotten corner of Alipur, its weathered exterior a testament to the passage of time.

The sky overhead was a canvas of darkened clouds, casting a somber pall over the city below. Though no rain fell, the threat lingered in the air, mirroring the uncertainty that weighed heavily on Sunjay and Sunita's hearts.

Arriving at the restaurant promptly at 6 pm, the couple opted for an outdoor table, seeking solace in the seclusion it offered. As they settled into their seats, their minds raced with the weight of the conversation that awaited them.

"What approach should we take, Sunita?" Sunjay mused, his voice tinged with uncertainty. "How do we broach this delicate matter with Jatinder?"

Sunita's response was measured, her voice a soothing balm amidst the turmoil. "We must remain calm and dignified," she advised, her words a reflection of her unwavering resolve. "There is no right or wrong way to approach this situation. We can only speak our truth and hope that Jatinder understands."

Her thoughts drifted to their own tumultuous past, the memory of their elopement casting a long shadow over their present predicament. "I remember the pain of trying to reconcile with my own family," she reminisced, her voice tinged with sadness. "But times have changed, Sunjay. The younger generation is more independent, more inclined to forge their own path."

As they awaited Jatinder's arrival, the tension in the air was palpable, each passing moment laden with anticipation. Suddenly, the sound of approaching footsteps drew their attention, and they turned to greet their guest with a mixture of trepidation and relief.

Their hearts quickened as they beheld Jatinder's familiar form, his presence a reminder of the weighty task that lay before them. Rising to their feet, Sunjay enveloped him in a warm embrace, while Sunita greeted him with a heartfelt hug, her eyes betraying the concern that lay within.

As they settled into conversation, the words flowed freely between them, each moment fraught with emotion as they navigated the delicate balance of tradition and individual autonomy. And amidst the swirling currents of uncertainty, one thing remained clear: no matter the outcome, they would face it together, bound by the ties of love and family that transcended time and circumstance.

Sunjay hugged him, and Sunita gave him a hug. "Welcome, my child," Sunjay said, "How are you, beta?"

"I am well," he said, "Just been busy with work and the family. How are you all?"

"We are well," Sunjay replies. The waiter soon approaches the table and asks what they would like as an appetizer. Sunjay asks Jatinder to choose, and he said something light is fine.

"Is pakora okay with you?" Jatinder asked.

"Yes," they both replied. The three of them chatted for 10-15 minutes about general things like politics and Jatinder's business and work. After they had drunk the tea and eaten the pakora, Sunjay sighed a long sigh and said, "Jatinder, you are probably wondering why we called you here tonight?"

"Yes," he said, "I was wondering."

"Well there is no easy way to say this, but we are here to bring you bad news, to say the least," Sunjay said. Sunita then began to speak as well. She started off by saying that we were very happy when he and Nina got engaged. "However, there is no easy way to tell you this, Jatinder beta. Nina is declining to go through with the marriage," Sunita said quietly.

"We say this with heavy hearts," Sunita said. They both refrained from making eye contact with Jatinder. But Sunita then raised her head and decided she needed to face him when delivering the news. Jatinder remained poised as he tried to take in the news. He began to smirk and let out a long sigh. Sunjay then said, "We are so sorry to do this to you, but we had to let you know as soon as we were told. We are going to tell you the truth about the situation. The truth is that Nina has met a person that she feels a connection with and wants to pursue a relationship with him. She has no ill will towards you and your family, but she felt her destiny is with another person. We are both sorry to you and your family and felt we had to tell you this in person. Nina has been beside herself beta, but we cannot insist that she goes through with something she is not sure about."

The ambiance was cozy, with the soft hum of conversation mingling with the aroma of freshly brewed chai.

As the conversation turned to the delicate matter at hand, Jatinder's gaze flickered momentarily, his thoughts a tumultuous whirlwind of emotions. Yet, as he met Sunjay's steady gaze, his resolve solidified, and he spoke with a quiet strength that belied his inner turmoil.

"There is no need for apologies," Jatinder reassured them, his voice calm yet tinged with empathy. "Nina's decision to come forward speaks volumes about her character. She has shown immense courage and integrity."

His words echoed with a profound truth, resonating deeply within the hearts of Sunjay and Sunita. They listened intently as Jatinder shared his own struggles with the concept of arranged marriage, his candidness a testament to the complexities of tradition and modernity.

"I too have grappled with the expectations placed upon me," Jatinder admitted, his voice tinged with vulnerability. "There have been moments when I questioned whether the path laid out for me was truly my own. I have always wanted to travel the world and explore the many beautiful countries rather than getting married straight away."

As he spoke, the weight of his confession lifted, replaced by a sense of liberation. In that moment, amidst the shared vulnerability, a bond of understanding formed between them, transcending the boundaries of culture and tradition.

"I am grateful to be engaged to a woman of such strength and conviction," Jatinder continued, his words infused with admiration. "Nina's courage has inspired me to confront my own reservations and uncertainties about marriage."

A shared moment of levity broke the tension, laughter ringing out as Jatinder lightened the mood with a playful jest. Sunjay and Sunita exchanged a knowing glance, a silent acknowledgment of the newfound understanding that had blossomed between them.

As they bid farewell to Jatinder, his parting words echoed in their hearts, a reminder of the power of courage and conviction. "Please do not feel sorry for me," he urged, his tone lighthearted yet sincere. "This is all for the best, and I wish you and Nina nothing but happiness."

With a final embrace, Sunjay and Sunita watched as Jatinder disappeared into the bustling streets of Delhi, his words lingering in the air like a gentle breeze. And as they made their way home, a sense of peace settled over them, knowing that they had found a true friend in Jatinder, and that Nina was free to follow her heart.

After several weeks the parents met Arun and his family and were very impressed by them. Sunjay watched Arun every move and analyzed each and every conversation with him. When the entire family was together Sunjay smiled and nodded to Sunita as if to say that he approved of Arun. After the meeting Nina's parents gleed ear to ear and said that they were delighted with Arun and his family. After several hours had passed the doorbell rang, Nina was surprised ,are we were expecting someone she asked her father. Yes beta Pandit Ji called this morning and said that he wanted to come by and spend the evening with us. The servant answered the door and touched the feet of the pandit, an Indian tradition of respect.Nina was very surprised but very pleased to see him. She greeted him with open arms and a huge smile. Nina looked at her mother for answers as to why he was there, Sunita whispered to her daughter we had contacted the pandit to see if this was a good match for you. Well Pandit Ji said it was an excellent match and you will have a very happy life together. Nina embraced her mother and held her emerald necklace close to her chest. When the evening was over the family said their goodbyes and when Nina went to thank the pandit for all his help, he smiled and again pointed to the sky. Remember child only those who have faith in the almighty are helped. We have to allow god into our hearts and pray, and only then will he assist us. Nina's family agreed and thanked him again.

For Nina, the journey towards freedom had been a long and arduous one, fraught with uncertainty and doubt. Yet, as she looked upon her parents with fresh eyes, she saw not just authority figures, but individuals who had faced their own battles with courage and resilience.

Their decision to elope in their youth had been a revelation, shedding light on the depths of their love and the sacrifices they had made for one another. It was a story of defiance in the face of tradition, a testament to the power of love to transcend all obstacles.

As the sun dipped below the horizon, casting a warm glow over the rocky terrain of Delhi, Nina and Arun stepped off the train hand in hand, their hearts filled with a newfound sense of freedom and possibility. For the first time, they could openly declare their love for one another, unburdened by the chains of tradition and expectation. And as they walked hand in hand into the embrace of the city, they knew that their journey was just beginning, a journey filled with endless possibilities and the promise of a love that knew no bounds. While the cool breeze swept Nina's hair from side to side, she smiled at Arun lovingly. "We are free, my dear Nina, to conquer the world," Arun said with conviction, "Our love will forever give us strength to overcome any adversity God will send our way. There is no other stronger emotion than love, which overcomes anything. Let us start our new chapter." With hands held tightly Arun whispered to Nina, "Our love is no longer forbidden."

Caste has no bar

Societal change is often met with resistance, and the journey towards racial and gender equality has been no exception. Similarly, addressing inequality within the caste system is crucial. As Arun and Nina's wedding day drew near, they became absorbed in the dazzling colors and deep-rooted traditions of Indian culture, each moment celebrating the richness of their combined heritage.

In the bustling city of Mebrayli, Delhi, where the ancient streets echoed with the whispers of centuries past, Arun and Nina's families came together to celebrate the union of two souls destined to defy convention. Amidst the bustling bazaars and bustling thoroughfares, the air was alive with the scent of spices and the sound of laughter, a testament to the joyous occasion at hand.

Against this backdrop of bustling activity, Arun and Nina partook in a series of pre-wedding ceremonies, each one a reflection of the vibrant tapestry of Indian traditions. From the raucous beats of the dhol to the soul-stirring melodies of the sitar, the air was alive with the sounds of celebration, a symphony of joy that echoed through the streets of Mebrayli. The wedding venue, nestled amidst the verdant hillsides of Mebrayli, was a temple steeped in history and tradition, its ancient walls bearing witness to countless ceremonies and rituals that had unfolded within its sacred confines. It was here that Arun had spent his childhood, forging a bond with the priests who presided over the temple's hallowed grounds.

For Nina, the highlight of these festivities was the ritual of applying mehndi, intricate designs adorning her hands and feet with symbols of love and prosperity. With each delicate stroke of the henna paste, she felt a surge of excitement, her anticipation for the wedding day growing with each passing moment.

Meanwhile, Arun underwent the traditional cleansing ritual with turmeric paste, his skin bathed in the golden glow of this ancient tradition. As the paste was applied to his skin, he felt a sense of purification wash over him, cleansing him of any doubts or fears that lingered in his heart.

The wedding venue, nestled amidst the verdant hillsides of Mebrayli, was a temple steeped in history and tradition, its ancient walls bearing witness to countless ceremonies and rituals that had unfolded within its sacred confines. Here, amidst the lush greenery and fragrant blooms, Arun and Nina's love would be sanctified in the eyes of the divine.

Unlike many other temples, which adhered strictly to the dictates of caste and social hierarchy, this temple embraced the union of Arun and Nina with open arms. Here, amidst the flickering flames of the oil lamps and the scent of incense wafting through the air, they would exchange their vows, their love blessed by the gods themselves.

As they sat before the holy granth sahib, the sacred book of prayers, Arun and Nina felt a sense of peace wash over them, knowing that their love was blessed by the divine. And as Pandit Ram, a revered figure in the community, stood before them to officiate the ceremony, his words resonated with wisdom and compassion, reminding them of the timeless truths that transcended the boundaries of caste and creed. Drawing upon his decades of experience as a spiritual leader, Pandit Ram emphasized the inherent equality of all human beings, regardless of their caste or social standing. He spoke of the need to dismantle the barriers that had long divided society, urging his listeners to embrace a future where love and respect transcended the narrow confines of tradition. In history no equality was ever embraced without struggle, for example race and gender quality. These struggles for equality and the battle to dismantle systemic barriers and discrimination came about through persistence and tolerance for change. We need to fight for such equality within our caste system also.

With each word he spoke, Pandit Ram reaffirmed the sanctity of their love, urging them to embrace a future where love and acceptance reigned supreme. And as Arun and Nina exchanged their vows amidst the ancient walls of the temple, they knew that their love would endure for eternity, a testament to the enduring power of love to overcome all obstacles. And as he concluded his speech with the simple yet profound declaration that "caste has no bar" in the eyes of the divine, there was not a dry eye in the house, for in that moment, the barriers of caste and prejudice crumbled before the power of love.